PUFFIN BOOKS

CRUMMY MUMMY AND ME

It's not easy being the only sensible one in the family. Minna's forever having to nag her Mum. If she didn't, nothing would ever get done: the dentist appointments would get forgotten, the Giro would all be spent on glitter clothes, the goldfish bowl would never get cleaned out. Mum would just sit on the sofa with her boyfriend Crusher Maggot, watching the video and munching crisps. And how would *you* feel if your mother had royal-blue hair and wore tarantula earrings?

Minna's vain attempts to restrain her eccentric Mum, her disapproving Gran, the kindly (despite appearances) Crusher and her mischievous baby sister, make hilariously entertaining reading.

Anne Fine was born and educated in the Midlands and now lives in Edinburgh with her two daughters and an assortment of pets. She has written numerous highly acclaimed and prize-winning books for children and teenagers. Her novel *Goggle-Eyes* won the *Guardian* Children's Fiction Award and the Carnegie Medal, and her book *Bill's New Frock* won the Smarties Prize.

CRUMMY MUMMY AND ME

AND ME

by ANNE FINE

illustrations by
DAVID HIGHAM

PUFFIN BOOKS

for
FRAN WARREN
because it was her idea in the first place

PUFFIN BOOKS

Published by the Penguin Group
Penguin Books Ltd, 27 Wrights Lane, London W8 5TZ, England
Penguin Books USA Inc., 375 Hudson Street, New York, New York 10014, USA
Penguin Books Australia Ltd, Ringwood, Victoria, Australia
Penguin Books Canada Ltd, 10 Alcorn Avenue, Toronto, Ontario, Canada M4V 3B2
Penguin Books (NZ) Ltd, 182–190 Wairau Road, Auckland 10, New Zealand

Penguin Books Ltd, Registered Offices: Harmondsworth, Middlesex, England

First published by Marilyn Malin Books in association with André Deutsch Limited 1988
Published in Puffin Books 1989
9 10 8

Printed in England by Clays Ltd, St Ives plc
Filmset in Palatino

CONTENTS

1
CRUMMY MUMMY

I don't think my mum's fit to be a parent, really I don't. Every morning it's the same, every single morning. I'm standing by the front door with my coat on, ready to go. School starts at nine and it's already eight-forty or even later, and she's not ready. She's not even nearly ready. Sometimes she isn't even dressed.

"Come *on*," I shout up the stairs. "We have to leave now."

"Hang on a minute!"

"What are you *doing* up there?"

Her voice comes, all muffled, through the bedroom door:

"Nothing."

"You *must* be doing something," I yell.

"I'm *not*."

"Come down, then. We're *waiting*."

"Can't find my shoes."

I lean against the front door, sighing. With as much patience as I can muster, I call upstairs:

"Where did you take them off?"

"I *thought* I took them off in the bathroom . . ."

"Look there, then."

"I *have*."

"If you would only put your shoes away neatly at night, we wouldn't have to go through this every single morning!"

By now, of course, my baby sister's fretting. She's strapped inside her pushchair and since I put her coat and bonnet on at least ten minutes ago, and she's still indoors, her head and ears are getting hot and scratchy. She's boiling up into one of her little rages. Already she's trying to tug her bonnet off.

"Will you come *on*?" I shout upstairs. (I'm really getting mad now.)

"I'm coming. I'm coming!"

"Well, hurry *up*!"

At last, she comes downstairs. And even then she's never dressed right. You'd think, honestly you would, that we didn't have any windows upstairs, the way she chooses what to wear. She certainly can't bother to look through them at the weather. She'll sail down in midwinter, when it's snowing, in a thin cotton frock with short puffy sleeves, and no woolly.

I have to be firm.

"You can't come out like that."

"Why not?"

"You just can't," I tell her, "You'll catch your death. It's snowing out there. It's *far* too cold for bare arms. You'll freeze."

"I'll put a coat on."

But I just stare at her until she goes back upstairs for a sweater. And even then she'll choose something quite unsuitable. She never dresses in the right sort of thing. She'd wear her glittery legwarmers to a funeral if I let her (or if we ever went to funerals). She'd sit on a beach in her thick purple poncho. If she were called in to see the headmaster, she'd rather wear those baggy flowery shorts she found abandoned on a park bench last Easter than anything sensible. She'd look fantastic – she always does – but not at all like a mother. You have to watch her. You can't let up.

At least she admits it.

"I'm a terrible embarrassment to you, Minna," she confesses, buckling on two of her best studded belts. "I'm a Crummy Mummy."

Then I feel mean for being so stern.

"You're not a Crummy Mummy," I tell her. "You do your best. And I suppose it doesn't *really* matter what you look like . . ."

"You're right," she says, cheering up at once. And then, if you let her, she'd get worse. At least, that's what my gran says, and she should know because she's her mother.

I like my gran. She lives right on the other side of the estate, but she comes over almost every tea-time. She picks Miranda out of the cot, and coos to her,

3

and then she sits with Miranda on her knee on the only bit of the sofa that isn't leaking stuffing. Mostly, she tells Mum off. She says now Mum's a mother of two, it's time she grew up and pulled herself together. She tells Mum she should throw all her safety-pin earrings and lavender fishnet tights into the dustbin, and go out and buy herself a nice, decent frock from Marks and Spencers. She says Mum ought to take those horrible Punk Skunks records off the stereo before they ruin Miranda, and put on something nice and easy to listen to, like Perry Como's Christmas Selection.

And then, if Mum hasn't already flounced off in a huff, Gran purses her lips together as if she's been sucking lemons and, clutching Miranda so tightly her dummy pops out of her mouth and her face goes purple, she whispers to Mum that she's clearly still very much under the influence of that dreadful, *dreadful* –

Here, she looks around shiftily, and drops her voice even lower:

"I don't even want to say his *name* in front of innocent children, but you know exactly who I mean."

I know exactly who she means, too. She means Crusher Maggot, that's who she means.

Crusher Maggot is Mum's boyfriend. It was me who first called him Crusher Maggot because that's what he looks like, and when he first started coming round here I didn't like him. Now I like him a lot, but it's too late. The nickname's stuck. He doesn't mind, though. And now even Mum calls him Crusher Maggot.

Gran disapproves of Crusher. She thinks he's a very bad influence on Mum. She blames him for giving Miranda her nickname – Crummy Dummy – and she particularly hates his hair. She says it's a hideous embarrassment.

Crusher's hair is fantastic. He even won a punk hair competition with it once, and his photo ended up on one of those London postcards that tourists send home to their friends for a laugh. The postcard was called *London's Burning*. And there's our Crusher, teeth bared, eyes staring, his hair in flaming red and orange spikes, scowling horribly at the photographer. We've got it propped up on the mantelpiece Gran hates the sight of it.

But, then again, when Crusher goes to all the trouble of shaving his head, Gran doesn't like that any better. She doesn't like his tattoo. I've even heard her telling our next-door neighbours how common she thinks it is. And they agreed. (They're not keen on Crusher, either. They don't like the noise his car makes when it starts – *if* it starts. They say it wakes their children.)

Personally, I rather like Crusher's tattoo. It only shows up when his head is freshly shaved. It says MADE IN BIRMINGHAM, and Crusher claims he was – well, on the outskirts. And we don't see it all that often anyway, because whenever he's gone to the trouble of dyeing his hair a different colour, he lets the spikes grow out all over.

Crusher dyes his hair pretty often, considering. Since the postcard, he's been green and pink, yellow and purple. Right now, he's blue. Gran and he had a row about it only last week. Crusher just happened to stroll into the kitchen while Gran was tipping breakfast plates into the sink and washing them, so we could start on tea. Mum was upstairs, doing something in the bathroom, no one knew what, but it was using up all the hot water, Gran said. And I was giving Crummy Dummy her bottle.

"Wotcha, Granny," Crusher greeted her cheerily. "I hope one of those plates you're rinsing is for me."

He's ever so friendly, is Crusher Maggot. I can't think why Gran just can't get used to him, like I did. But she can't. She spun round at the draining-board and glowered at him before saying tartly:

"You've got your feet well and truly under the table, haven't you, young Maggot?"

Baffled, Crusher looked down at his Doc Martins. But Gran kept on at him. She's good at nagging, Gran is. (Mum says that I take after her.)

"Look at your hair!" Gran snorted. "It's sky-blue! It's dreadful the way you amble around this estate looking like something that fell off the wall at the Modern Art Gallery. I'm horrified that a daughter of mine is prepared even to be seen walking along the street beside someone with hair that shocking colour!"

"Your hair is blue, too," argued Crusher. He was hurt. "You had that perm and rinse and set only last week. Your hair is definitely blue."

"A faint bluish tinge, maybe," Gran said, blushing hotly. "Not sky-blue!"

"Not royal blue, either!" I cried. For Mum had just sailed into the kitchen. And her hair was royal blue! It was the brightest, deepest, richest blue I ever saw. It was bluer than winter afternoons, bluer than the leggings Gran knitted for Crummy Dummy, bluer even than Sophie Howard's gown when she played the Virgin Mary in our Nativity play last year.

Gran stared. I stared. Crusher stared. Even Crummy Dummy stared. Then Gran and Crummy Dummy both burst into tears.

"Waaaah!" screamed Crummy Dummy, and she stretched out her arms desperately to me, hoping I would protect her from this blue-topped stranger.

"Aaaaagh!" shrieked poor Gran, holding her hand over her heart. Gingerly, she stuck out a finger and prodded one of Mum's spikes.

"How can you do this to your old mother?" she wailed. "A girl's hair is supposed to be her crowning glory! Royal-blue hair! *Royal-blue hair*! What will the neighbours think? Answer me that!"

"They'll think she looks fair smashing," said

Crusher. "And that she matches the paintwork on my car."

You could tell Gran was shocked. She went pale as a grub.

"I'm warning you two," she said in her dangerous

voice. "You're going too far. A mother can only stand *so much*."

(This interested me. A lot. For I suspect my mum can stand almost any amount. It's me who cracks. That's why I have a lot of natural sympathy for my gran.)

Gran shook her finger at Mum so hard that her new perm and set wobbled on her head like a pale-blue jelly.

"If you stay royal blue, I shall disown you. Yes, I shall. I won't come round here any more. I won't babysit for you when you go down to the disco with this – this *barbarian* here" (pointing at Crusher, who looked hurt again). "I won't talk to you. I'll even cut you dead in the street. You have to choose. Royal-blue hair, or your own mother!"

There was a horrible silence. Nobody moved. Nobody spoke. Mum just looked sulky.

Gran turned to me. Prising Crummy Dummy out of my arms, she placed a kiss upon her forehead.

"Farewell, sweet babe," she said. "I hope for your sake that your mother sees sense, and we are not parted for too long."

I got a kiss and a speech too.

"Goodbye, Minna dear," she said. "I know it can be hard when a mother puts maggots before the family."

I had some sympathy with that, as well. I've thought it often enough myself, when Mum and Crusher are too wrapped up in giggling together about something silly to pay any attention to me.

"'Bye, Gran," I said. "I, too, hope our parting won't last for long."

It did, though. It lasted for days. Gran never

visited once. I was pretty upset, I can tell you. I missed her coming over every afternoon and asking me about what happened at school, and helping me with my spelling homework. And Crummy Dummy missed her too, you could tell. She took to sitting forlornly with her dummy in her mouth, looking all miserable and deprived.

On Wednesday, we caught sight of Gran for the first time since the quarrel. She was stepping out of Mr Hamid's shop carrying a bagful of vegetables just as we came over the pedestrian walkway to the shopping centre. I waved and shouted at her through the railings; but since I was with Mum, Gran ignored me and swept off under the concrete arches extremely grandly, like the Queen Mother, pretending she hadn't heard me call.

"See where your stubbornness has led us?" I scolded Mum, as Gran disappeared between Vikki's Video Palace and the boarded-up wool shop.

Mum said something rude. I shan't repeat it. But I persisted in trying to reason with her.

"Is it worth it, just for blue hair?"

"Ask her, not me," snapped Mum, and pulled me after the pushchair so sharply she practically wrenched my arm out of its socket.

So I asked her. I asked Gran the very next time that I bumped into her, picking her way around the muddy patch of the shortcut across the recreation ground.

I spread my hands out in what the author of my *Best Bible Stories* always refers to as "a beseeching fashion".

"Is it worth it, Gran, just for blue hair?" I cried.

What Gran said was almost as rude as what Mum

10

said. I shan't repeat that, either. But I confess to being a little shocked. She is my granny, after all.

I left the two of them to it, after that. I knew the problem couldn't last for ever because Crusher had told me Mum's blue was the sort that washed out. So I concentrated my efforts on cheering Crummy Dummy, who didn't know that. I made Crusher fix up her baby-bouncer. It's not been right since Mum took off half the chain links to wear to a dance. And I made the hole in her bottle a whole lot bigger. She's been sucking and blowing like a smoker when the lift's broken, trying to get the milk out, poor thing. And I cut the feet off the ends of her stripy babygrow suit. I reckon her toes were getting all squashed up.

And I waited. But Gran never came, and Mum never even went next door to phone her. It was nearly a week.

"What a stubborn pair of bats!" was the only remark Crusher made about the whole sorry business.

And then, just as I was despairing, there came the night of the gale.

What a night that was! The rain beat down, lashing against the window panes till every dream turned into a nightmare. It was still dark at breakfast-time. Storm water was seeping under the kitchen door, and running over the lino in rivulets. The wind was so fierce it would have had Crummy Dummy's bonnet off in a flash, if I hadn't insisted Mum leave her with old Mrs Pitopoulos next door, instead of dragging her out in the pushchair.

"I don't *need* chumming to school," I told Mum when she was still scouring the cupboards hopelessly for her scarlet plastic bosun's helmet at seven minutes to nine. "You don't *have* to come with me."

"You don't *have* to go," she countered irritably.

"I do," I insisted. "It's a schoolday, isn't it? I'm not sick, or injured, am I?"

"Don't push your luck, Minna," she said, climbing into her wellies and scowling.

So we set off to school through the gale. You've never seen anything like it. The street was absolutely clean! All of the litter had been washed away – even the tatty old cardboard boxes outside number twelve, and those great lengths of stair carpet on the corner that the dustbin men have refused for four whole weeks to shove into their mechanical chewer.

The main road was amazing, too. Cars were crawling along with their drivers hunched forward and peering through little arcs on the windscreens. The tyres hurled wide sheets of filthy gutter water up in our faces. Mum spat and cursed. Her wellies were flooded.

And just at that moment, I noticed Gran. She was staggering out of her cul-de-sac, into the wind, fighting her umbrella which looked just as though it were fighting her back.

I squeezed Mum's arm.

"Look," I said, pointing. "Gran! And we're going the same way."

Mum blinked raindrops off her eyelashes, and looked. Then she shouted to me over the wind:

"I'm not slowing up. Not in this weather. And now I'm this wet, I'm not going back either."

And, with that, she strode on with her head down against the spiteful winds and the rain.

Gran was striding along, almost beside us. She clearly had the same idea. The weather was far too awful to slow up, or take a longer route, or go back home and set off again later. She was going to brazen it out, just like Mum.

The two of them were practically side by side now, each striding along into the wind, and neither of them so much as giving one tiny little sideways peep at the other.

And that was their big mistake! For the oddest thing was happening. The strangest sight! Both of them were changing. It was almost as if the storm were playing its own little private joke on the pair of them.

Mum's hair was changing back to its normal colour! First, little streaks started running like tiny bright-blue rivers down her cheeks, over her ears, and down the back of her neck. Her hair was gradually returning to mousey-brown, the colour it was before she went royal blue. The dye was washing out, faster and faster. And the spikes were collapsing. The wind was blowing them flat. Mum didn't notice, but by the time we reached the corner, she looked as clean and neat and tidy as she does in the photo that was taken of her at convent school.

(Gran loves that photo. She keeps it on the mantelpiece at her house in a special fur frame. Mum says it makes her look like a wally, and slams it down on its face whenever we visit. If the frame wasn't fur, she'd have smashed it by now, doing that.)

And Mum wasn't the only one looking different. Gran was changing, too. As she marched into the same fierce wind, her neat little parting was whipped away, and patches of her hair stuck up in clumps, like Crusher's after his football practice. Her hair was wet, too, making the blue look bluer. Gran no longer looked like someone who'd been to the hairdresser only ten days ago. She looked like someone who'd been dragged backwards through a hedge.

Then, as we reached the school gates, the wind gave one last, amazing flourish. It whipped Gran's hair up into spikes. It whipped a nice neat parting into Mum's straight brown hair. And it whipped the umbrella clean out of Gran's grasp.

Mum reached out and caught the handle automatically, as it flew past. Then, since she couldn't think of anything else to do with it, she turned to Gran to hand it back.

Gran turned to her, to take it.

Both of them stared.

Gran stared at neat, sweet, tidy Mum, looking just like she used to look in her favourite photo on the mantelpiece.

Mum stared at punky, spiky, blue Gran, looking a bit like Crusher Maggot on a bad morning.

Tears came to Gran's eyes first.

"Look at you! You look *lovely!*" she cried, and reached out to give Mum one of her giant hugs.

"And you!" Mum squealed with pleasure, hugging her back. "You look smashing, just smashing!"

"What a wonderful surprise!"

"Oh, you are too! Really!"

I sighed, and shook my head. Then the school bell rang. I walked away, and neither of them even noticed. They were far too busy praising one another for their beautiful hairstyles.

It's a good job there are no mirrors hanging on our school wall, I reckoned. But you never know. . . . In my experience, most of their silly squabbles get sorted out in time, if you just ignore them.

2
A REALLY BORING RIDE IN THE COUNTRY

As soon as school finished, I ran straight home. Even though it was a beautiful day, Mum was inside, sitting on the sofa with Crusher Maggot, watching the video and munching crisps. Crummy Dummy was jumping up and down in her cot as usual, trying to bump her head on the ceiling.

I said hello to Crummy Dummy first.

"Hi, babe," I drawled in my American gangster voice. "How's life behind bars?"

She smiled and dribbled down her chin. She likes me so much. While I was tickling her tummy, I asked Mum:

"What are you watching?"

"Horror film," Mum said. "*Curse of the Blood of Dracula*. Pass the fizzy."

I knew she meant the bottle on the table because that was redcurrant, and redcurrant was the colour Crummy Dummy was dribbling. I don't care very much for it myself, and especially not while *Curse of the Blood of Dracula* is on the video. So I gave the bottle straight to Mum. She took a couple of swallows and passed it on to Crusher. He had a slug, then pushed the bottle between the cot bars.

"Here, Crummy Dummy," he said. "Have a swig."

I sighed. I do get a bit fed up with fighting the same old battles all the time.

"You really shouldn't let Crusher give that stuff to the baby," I told Mum.

Now Crusher sighed. You could tell that he thought I was nagging.

"Why not?" he asked.

"It rots her teeth."

"She hasn't any," Crusher argued.

"They're in there, growing," I insisted. "And drinking fizzy is a terrible habit." I turned to Mum. "You really shouldn't buy it," I told her. "It's full of sugar, colourants and additives. It has no goodness in it at all."

Now Mum was sighing as well. But, let's face it, it's not my fault that I'm for ever having to nag. Left to herself, she makes a terrible parent. If I'm not careful, she forgets all my visits to the dentist, and lets me stay up way past my bedtime, even on schoolnights, and never checks I've done my homework properly, or changed my socks. I think she ought to make more of an effort, really. I think she ought to run the house a bit better, and dress Crummy Dummy up in nicer clothes (and stop everybody calling her that – her name is Miranda!) I think she ought to buy wholemeal bread instead of white sliced, and take that safety pin out of her ear. I think she should stop being cheeky to the man from the welfare, and spending the giro on clothes that glitter, and bits for Crusher Maggot's old car.

And I don't think that I ought to come home from school on a beautiful afternoon to find her sitting in a darkened room, watching the video. There are far better things to do.

I didn't say anything, though. There was no point. The film was coming to an end, anyway. A very sticky end. A crush of flailing vampires was slowly drowning in what should have been the blood of Dracula, but looked more like orange squash because the colours on the telly have not been right since Crummy Dummy fiddled with the buttons.

Mum stretched, and opened the curtains.

"Game of cards, Minna?" she asked hopefully.

"I can't," I said. "I haven't done my homework yet."

"You could do it later."

"No, I can't," I told her firmly. "I want to go down to the launderette after tea. I'm out of socks."

Mum sighed. I don't think she finds me easy. I bet

she hopes Crummy Dummy grows up a bit different, more like her, not bothering about things like homework and clean teeth and matching socks, and ready to drop whatever she's doing to have a bit of fun. Because Mum is good fun, even if some of the neighbours do tighten up their lips when she strides past in silver boots, and the Health Visitor thinks she shouldn't have trimmed Crummy Dummy's hair into a mohican so soon, and I am always having to go on at her.

"Crusher? Fancy a game of cards?"

Crusher stood up, knocking a pile of crisp packets on to the carpet.

"No," he said. "I'm off to buy a bit for the car."

Mum looked around. Crummy Dummy was the only one left, but she can't play cards. She simply puts them in her mouth and sucks the edges till they're soggy.

"It's tea-time, anyway," I reminded Mum. "Better leave the cards till after."

"Oh, all right," Mum agreed. But I could see she didn't like it because she dragged her boot heels along the lino, following me into the kitchen. We were out of butter. And out of bread. And out of tea-bags. I had to borrow two pounds from the emergency tin, and leave Mum clattering the dirty breakfast plates off the table, while I went down to the shop.

And that's how it happened that no one was in the room when the television and the video were stolen. No one except Crummy Dummy, that is. And she didn't raise the alarm. She didn't even make a noise, Mum said. Not one squawk. She just sat there in her nappies and watched. Probably thought it was as good a show as any on the telly when the thief sneaked in through the open front door, past the kitchen where Mum was, and into the room, picking his way softly and carefully through all the crumpled crisp packets lying on the floor ready to crackle, lifting the telly and the video, and carrying them out without a sound. He even must have slipped a square of milk chocolate to Crummy Dummy through the cot bars on his way out. We found it dribbled down her, after.

Everyone realized what had happened at the same moment. Mum came out of the kitchen just as I came back from the shops and Crusher Maggot strolled in the back door.

"Hello," said Crusher. "Where's the telly?"

"And the video."

"Gone!"

"Who's taken them?"

"Have we had burglars?"

"What's going on?"

You can imagine the fuss. Mum nearly had a fit. Crusher was furious. The video belonged to him. He brought it round to our house months ago to tape the Cup Final, and never took it home again. I was just going to mention to Mum how silly it was of her not to have made sure we had proper insurance, when Crusher said:

"What about Crummy Dummy? She was here all the time. She must have seen whoever it was come in and steal them."

Mum lifted Crummy Dummy out of her cot and tried to get her to spill the beans; but since she can only say *bokkle* and *bye-bye* and *tac* (that's cat backwards), it wasn't any use. Mum soon gave up.

"I suppose we'll have to phone the police," she said.

"Police?" said Crusher. He didn't sound too keen. But Mum went off next door in her silver boots to borrow their phone. Crusher sat, sunk in gloom, facing the empty space and bare wall that used to be our television and his video. I didn't mind too much.

I only watch the nature programmes and the documentaries. And I'm beginning to suspect that television kills conversation.

Crusher's conversation was none too interesting. All he kept saying was:

"If I find out who it was, I'll rip his ears off."

The police, when they finally turned up, didn't seem bothered. (Of course, it wasn't their telly or their video.) There were two of them, one old, one young. The old one said this sort of thing happens all the time in an area like ours. He didn't hold out much hope for our getting the things back. He hadn't anyone spare at the moment to send out looking. Crusher glared at him then, as much as to say: "You're not doing all that much yourself, are you, just standing here gassing. Why don't *you* go out looking?" But the old one didn't notice, and the young one was just leaning against the draining-board staring at Mum. You could tell that he disapproved of her and fancied her at the same time. So could the old one. He took him off.

Two seconds after they'd gone, Crusher flung himself face down on the sofa, and beat the cushions with his fists.

"No!" he howled. "No! Tonight! At ten o'clock! The Snooker Final!"

Great chunks of sponge kept shooting out of the cushions. Poor Crusher was beside himself. Mum and I tried desperately to think of something to distract him.

"We could take that nice walk along the deserted railway line," I suggested. "It would do Crummy Dummy good to get some fresh air, and there are some smashing wild flowers beside the track."

Mum pretended to throw up in Crusher's old wellies.

"All right," I said crossly. "*You* think of something."

She thought of something.

"A ride. A ride in Crusher's car."

"Where?"

"Down the dog track?" Mum suggested hopefully.

"No," I insisted. "Somewhere nice. In the country."

"*Bor*ing," said Mum. "Really *bor*ing." But I'd made up my mind. And Mum was too busy trying to get Crusher Maggot to pull himself together to argue for long enough to wear me down.

So off to the country we went in Crusher's car. It's a real crate. Crusher says the reason it's bare and rusty in patches all over is because it's such a good car that it's worth saving up for a proper respray. It eats up petrol and it won't go fast. Crusher says that's a "sophisticated design safety feature", but Mum and I think it's because the gearstick's bent and Crusher can't force it into fourth gear. We wouldn't dare to say so, though. He'd stop the car and make us walk.

We bowled along. Nobody overtook us. (The roads were quite empty. "They're all at home, getting ready to watch the snooker," Crusher said bitterly.) Trees flashed by on either side. ("It's nice to go at a speed where Crummy Dummy can see the birds clearly," I said to Mum.) The petrol-gauge hovered on full. (Then, prising her boots off, Mum caught the glass in front of it by mistake with her heel, and the needle dropped suddenly to halfway-empty.)

"This *was* a good idea," Mum said, stifling a yawn.

And that was when Crummy Dummy screeched.

"*Greee-eee-eee-eee!*"

You've never heard a noise like it. It was worse than the howl Mum let out the day she spilt green nail polish all down her new sequinned tracksuit.

Crusher threw his foot on to the brake. The car lurched to a halt in the middle of nowhere.

"What on *earth*. . . ?"

Crummy Dummy was bouncing up and down so hard that her nappy was squelching.

"*Greee-eee-eee-eee!*"

"What's the matter with her?"

"Maybe she's got a pin stuck in her."

"Of course she hasn't." I was hurt. "I put that nappy on her."

She did it again.

"*Greee-eee-eee-eee!*"

"She's all excited about something."

"What's she looking at?"

"Nothing."

"She must be looking at something. Her eyes are open."

I craned my neck round beside hers, to try to see what she was looking at.

"She's looking at that hill over there."

"What hill?"

"That hill."

"That boring old hill? That's nothing special."

So Crusher put the car back into gear. We'd hardly gone a couple of feet before:

"*Greee-eee-eee-eee!*"

The same noise again, as piercing as one of those whistling kettles, and Crummy Dummy struggling like mad.

Crusher was getting irritated.

"What's the matter with her?"

"It's just that hill. She's staring at that hill."

We all stared through the car windows. Outside was a huge hill, green with pines in places and bare in others where they'd chopped them down.

"Why would she stare at that?" asked Crusher, mystified. "It's about as exciting a scene as the test card on telly. One great big boring hill, covered in patches of boring pointy pine trees in boring straight rows, with boring zig-zag cart tracks between them."

"I bet that was a nice hill once," said Mum. "Before the Forestry Commission got at it, and turned it into a matchstick factory."

"*Greee-eee-eee-eee!*" Bounce, bounce, bounce. A nice quiet ride in the country? Some hopes.

"She's trying to tell us something," I said.

"What?"

"I don't know, do I? But I know she is."

We all stared at the hill. Suddenly Mum's eyes began to glaze over.

"It's starting to remind me of something," she said.

"What is?"

"That hill."

"That hill!" Crusher was getting really impatient now. "How can a boring old hill covered in spiky little Lego trees with zig-zags all over remind you of anything?"

"I don't know," Mum said. "But it does."

So we all sat and stared some more. Then Crusher said:

"Me too. It's beginning to remind me of something."

I shook my head. I thought they were both crazy. Until –

"Me too! Me too! But, don't you see?" I shouted. "Don't you see? It's not *something* it reminds you of at all. It's *someone*!"

"Someone?"

"Don't understand."

"Look again!" I said excitedly. "Look!"

They all looked again, except for Crummy Dummy, who hadn't taken her eyes off the hill, or stopped screeching and bouncing, from the very first moment we drove round the corner and saw it.

The hill was round. Sort of head-shaped. The little pointy trees stuck all over it looked just like green-dyed spikes of hair on a punk's head. The fire-breaks looked like zig-zag partings. The longer you sat and looked at the hill, the more it looked like someone, someone punk, someone with green hair and zig-zag partings.

"The thief must look just like that hill," I said. "That's what Crummy Dummy is trying to tell us. She got a good look at him through the cot bars."

"She'd not forget anyone who feeds her chocolate," Crusher said. "Crummy Dummy has a passion for chocolate."

"She shouldn't even know what it tastes like," I scolded. (Sometimes I think I'm fighting a losing battle.)

"I'm driving straight back into town," Crusher said. "And if I see anyone who looks like that hill over there, carrying a telly or a video, he'd better watch out for his ears."

He sounded as if he meant it, too.

He turned the car around – a neat, nine-point turn – and we went back, Crummy Dummy all twisted round in her car seat, screeching loudly in my ears, flapping her arms desperately towards the hill we were leaving behind.

Almost as soon as we got back to town we spotted him, staggering down the great long strip of wasteland beside the ring road. We all guessed it was him straight away, except for Crummy Dummy who had fallen asleep. He had patches of thick pine-green hair and patches of stubble stuck anyhow all over his head, together with zig-zag partings. And he was carrying two enormous cardboard boxes, one on top of the other. They must have been terribly heavy. Every few yards he put them down to rest his arms.

Crusher pulled up the car and he and Mum both jumped out. I followed a bit more slowly because I was carrying Crummy Dummy and didn't want to wake her in case she went back to screeching again.

Crusher stood right in front of the fellow, and tapped the cardboard boxes with his fingers.

"What have you got in there, mate?" he asked. "Mind if I take a butcher's?"

The man said something rude. I shan't repeat it.

Crusher Maggot said darkly:

"I think that what you've got in there is my video and –", pointing at Mum, "this good lady's television."

"Prove it," the man said.

"You're on," Crusher said. "The telly has redcurrant juice smeared all over the screen, and the buttons on the video are sticky with sherbert."

"You've *never* been giving her sherbert!" I cried. (Now I was really angry.)

The man looked a bit desperate.

"I might have spilled redcurrant down my own screen," he argued.

"And sherbert on your buttons?" Crusher scoffed.

The fellow blushed, and fell silent.

Just then, Crummy Dummy woke up. Recognizing the man who fed her chocolate, she tried to throw herself out of my arms into his, squealing with pleasure. I very nearly dropped her.

"That settles it," said Mum. "She knows who you are."

There was a squeal of brakes behind us. The two policemen we met earlier had drawn up at the kerb in their car. Mum thought she heard the young one say, "Evening, Boots," as he wound down the window. She was just going to step over and tell him off when Crusher whispered something about his tax disc, and she decided not to bother.

"Anything wrong?" the older policeman asked curiously.

"I don't think so, thank you very much, officer," Crusher returned politely. "This gentleman here is just helping me load a couple of boxes into my car." He turned to the thief. "Aren't you?" he asked, equally politely.

"Yes," said the thief hastily. "Yes, I am. Sir."

The young policeman got out and opened the top box.

"You can't last long without a telly, can you?" he said. Then he winked at Mum, got back in the car, and they drove off.

Crusher said to the thief.

"Hurry up. We'll be missing the snooker."

The thief packed the two boxes as neatly as he could into the boot of Crusher's car.

"Going our way?" Mum offered, forgetting.

"No, he's not," Crusher said, not forgetting.

We drove off home, in good time for the snooker in spite of being in third gear. Mum made a special tea, and though the cake was stuffed with colourants and additives, I didn't say a word, not even when they gave some to Crummy Dummy.

I reckoned she'd earned it, really I did.

3
OUR PET

This story's not a pleasant one, but I think that it should be told. Those of you with a nervous disposition (that means all the ones who end up face down on the bed sobbing their hearts out after watching something really sad on the telly) should miss this story out. So should the very squeamish. You lot can leave now, and join us again at the beginning of the next chapter.

The rest can carry on reading, secure in the knowledge that I have asked Mr Higham to act as responsibly as possible about the illustrations.

Here we go, then.

One day, we were all sitting in the garden – well, my half of it. Nobody sane would want to sit in Mum's half. It's a pit. Old cans, bus tickets, empty bottles and torn crisp packets. Bits of old newspapers and one of Crusher's cast-off car tyres. Weeds. Stones. Two halves of a smashed sink. The whole patch is disgusting. (And *she's* at home all day. You might think, out of the two of us, she'd be the one to find the time to keep her half tidy. You'd be mistaken.)

My half's quite nice, I think. I have grass in the

middle, and grow petunias and pansies around my
edges. I'm not particularly struck on either flower,
but they came up well the first year I tried them, so
I've kept on with them. If you sit in my bit, and keep

your back to the rest, it can be pleasant in the garden, unless the wind is blowing old sweet wrappers across from Mum's side into your face and hair.

I could clear her half up, I suppose. I have thought about it. But part of me believes she'll never learn to take responsibility for her own messes if other people are forever picking up after her. She should be forced to face the consequences of her behaviour. She has to learn the hard way that if she doesn't bother to tend her half of the garden, it will become a rubbish dump.

And it has.

The only problem is, she doesn't seem to notice.

"*Isn't* it nice?" she said, stretching out half on my patch and half on hers. "I *love* gardens in summer."

Her sprawled-out body took up most of my carefully tended pocket-handkerchief lawn, and her head rested comfortably just on the edge of her patch, pillowed by Crusher's abandoned car tyre.

Crummy Dummy's pram was taking up most of the rest of my half, so Crusher and I squatted rather uncomfortably round the edges. He had his foot on one of my striped petunias, but I couldn't blame him. There was almost no room, unless he wanted to back into Mum's half, and take his chances among the old tin cans and bits of broken glass.

He was restless, anyhow. He kept stretching up and peering over the gate.

"What are you looking for?" I asked.

"There's someone coming round to see the car today," said Crusher. "A Mr Willoughby. I don't want to miss him. I'm hoping he'll buy it."

"It doesn't go," I pointed out. "Not since you left

33

the bonnet up through that great thunderstorm. Why should this Mr Willoughby pay for a car that doesn't go?"

"I've fixed it," Crusher said. "It goes."

"Once round the block," scoffed Mum. "*If* you're lucky."

"He's not expecting a Mercedes Benz," Crusher said coldly. "He's only paying seventy pounds."

"Seventy pounds?" Mum lifted her head and started peering over the gate as well. "Just think what we could do with seventy pounds!"

And it was because we were all peering over the gate in search of this saviour who was going to bring us seventy pounds that none of us noticed the horrible, mangy, disgusting old dog sneaking through a hole in the hedge behind us, and starting to do its business in our garden.

I saw it first. I was livid. I ran towards the foul, revolting thing, clapping and shouting and flapping my arms. But it didn't stop. It just kept squatting there, the scruffy, loathsome creature, and carried on till it was quite finished.

I lost my temper.

"Get out!" I shrieked. "Get out! *Get out*! GET OUT!"

"You really can't blame it," Crusher pointed out. "In all fairness, that half of the garden does look like a corporation tip. The poor creature probably believes he's chosen a socially acceptable place to perform."

"I think he's *sweet*," said Mum. "Is he stray?"

And she reached out for his scabby, tufty, twisted old neck. He had no collar, of course, and so no tag.

"He *must* be stray," she said. "He's terribly thin."

34

"I hope you're going to wash your hands very thoroughly indeed now," I said to Mum.

She wasn't listening.

"Can we keep him?" she was asking.

"*Keep* him!" I was beside myself. "*Keep* him? That mangy, ancient thing! He ought to be put down!"

Mum was shocked, I could tell.

"Put down?"

"Yes, put down." I was furious. "He's absolutely repellent. He's probably crawling with germs and bristling with fleas. He's sure to be carrying all manner of diseases. You can practically *see* him festering. He's horrible. *Horrible!*"

"Wouldn't you like a nice pet?" asked Mum.

(Sometimes, I don't believe she hears *a word I say*.)

So then, of course, we ended up in one of those great arguments you get into about pets. I don't need to give you all the details, do I? You've all been through it, haven't you? You've heard it all a million times, I'm sure. I started sensibly enough by giving Mum about a hundred good reasons why we don't want a pet, and couldn't manage one if we did, and even if we could, this dog would be the worse pet we could get. I know you can work out most of the hundred reasons yourself, but I'll start you off with the first ten:

1. Mum would be bored with him within a week.
2. Dogs spread diseases. They are dirty.
3. Injections cost the earth.
4. He'd be alone too much in the daytime.
5. We live right by a busy road.

6. We can barely feed us; we can't feed him, too.
7. He'd tear up my half of the garden.
8. We couldn't go away on trips.
9. No one has time to walk him every day.
10. No one would want to clear up his mess.

etc . . . etc . . . etc . . .

"*I'll* walk him every day," said Mum. "*I'll* clear up any mess. Promise!"

(Honestly! Are *you* subjected to this sort of rubbish?)

"How can you *say* that?" I practically screamed. "How *can* you? When did *you* last clear out the goldfish bowl? Look at this garden you were so keen on at the start! Remember the yoga classes? You spent all that money on that orange and pink leotard, and stopped going after only two weeks! How can you look me in the eye and promise you'll care for this dog as long as he lives?"

"He won't live long," said Crusher. "Look at him. He's on his last legs."

We all looked at the dog. Crusher was right. He was practically a basket case already with his great drooping mildewed tail and his scraggy body, his chewed-up ears and his pathetic look.

"No," Crusher said, shaking his head gravely. "That dog won't live long."

(We were to remind him of this prediction of his, some time later.)

We were still staring at the dog when the catch on the gate rattled. We all swung round. It was the man who had come round to see Crusher's car.

Crusher was all over him in an instant. He was

desperate to sell the car. It had been nothing but trouble from the day he bought it.

"Come in, Mr Willoughby," he cried. "No trouble finding us, I hope? Come in and have a cup of coffee."

He shepherded Mr Willoughby into the house. Mum followed them. I looked around. The dog was digging a great hole among my petunias.

"Clear off!" I yelled. "Go home! Disappear!"

But the old mange-ball just curled up in one of Mum's two halves of smashed sink, and fell asleep.

I went inside.

Crusher was standing in the middle of the kitchen, fussing about the car keys. He couldn't find them. And Mr Willoughby was beginning to look just a little impatient.

"I haven't got very long," he warned.

"I had them only a few minutes ago," cried Crusher, mystified. "They were right here, in my pocket!"

Mr Willoughby glanced at his watch.

"They're somewhere here!" said Crusher. "They *must* be!"

"Can't buy a car without a little test drive," said Mr Willoughby.

Crusher was desperate. He was whirling about, looking on all the shelves and table-tops, patting his body in search of a telltale bulge.

"Minna!" he said. "Look round the garden, will you, in case I happened to drop them there."

Now I'll give Crusher Maggot his due. He doesn't order me about much. (A lot less than I order him about, anyhow.) He doesn't take advantage of the fact that he's grown-up and I'm not, and he's with my mum. He doesn't tell me to do things as if he were my own father, which he's not. He doesn't push his luck.

So when he does ask me to do something, I usually try to cooperate.

"Just car keys, is it?" I asked.

"That's right," said Crusher. "On that plastic key ring – the one that looks like a bone."

Looks like a bone? Looks like a bone!

"That dog," I said, "was digging a hole in my petunias a few minutes ago."

And I went out to have a look.

I was right. We found the keys in no time at all. The dog hadn't buried them very far down. Perhaps he got bored, or maybe he was simply too lazy to bother to dig very deep. But there they were, anyway, a couple of inches under the surface, and still attached to the plastic bone key ring.

Crusher was delighted. He said to Mr Willoughby:

"I'll start the car up for you, and we'll go for a spin round the estate."

"*I'll* start the car," said Mr Willoughby. (Clearly

he was no slouch when it came to buying second-hand cars.)

"*I'll* start it," insisted Crusher. (Clearly he was no slouch at selling them, either.) "Backing out into this street is rather tricky."

Mr Willoughby was polite. He looked suspicious, but he didn't press the matter.

So that was how it came about that it was Crusher in the driving seat when the car backed out. Mr Willoughby stood beside Mum and me, watching, as Crusher slid in the car and pulled the safety belt over his shoulders. He switched on the ignition and started the engine.

It coughed straight into life. (Only Crusher can do it, and not all that often.)

"It starts well, doesn't it?" Mum said to Mr Willoughby, chattily.

Crusher pushed the gearstick into reverse and

released the handbrake. He looked in the mirror to check there was no traffic coming down the street, and then checked once again over his shoulder. He let the clutch up a little, and slowly, steadily, the car reversed.

Straight over the dog.

It had been lying curled up fast asleep behind the back wheel.

I'm not going to describe the scene. (I know you wouldn't want it.) Suffice it to say that, for the very first time since I had given it him, Crusher had well and truly lived up to his nickname.

Mum always knows exactly what to do in an emergency. She covered her face with her spread hands.

"Crusher," she said. "Fetch the coal-shovel right away."

"Minna," she said. "Run in the house and find one

of those nice big plastic rubbish bags for Crusher."

"Mr Willoughby," she said. "Come in the house with me and finish your coffee."

And, keeping her hands firmly over her face, she turned away, and Mr Willoughby obediently followed. As she strode to the back door, Crusher and I distinctly heard her saying:

"Fancy that poor old dog choosing a spot like that to lie down and die so naturally and peacefully in its sleep. We'll just bury it nicely. It won't take a moment. And then you can take the car out again."

Mr Willoughby was clearly too shaken to argue.

Crusher wielded the coal-shovel like a maniac. He was quite desperate not to lose his sale. Within three minutes he had dug a hole at least two feet deep. My poor petunias flew off the shovel in clumps.

"Why can't you bury the thing in Mum's patch?" I grumbled.

"You wait," he consoled me. "This is a natural fertilizer, this is. Next year your pansies will come up like sunflowers. You ought to plant a vine here, really."

I wasn't impressed.

As soon as Mum saw through the window that we were all cleared up, she ushered Mr Willoughby outside again, and Crusher ushered him inside the car. He was still dazed. He didn't even seem to notice how long it took him to start up the engine, and if he realized that awful clunking noise was coming from under the bonnet, he didn't say so.

In fact, he can't have been himself at all. He bought the car. He counted five ten-pound notes into Crusher's spread hand.

"I'm not paying a penny more than fifty," he warned.

"Done," Crusher agreed. "I'm really far too upset to argue."

And Mr Willoughby drove off in the car.

Crusher spun me round and round in his arms. (I knew he was ecstatic. Usually he says I'm far too big for that now, and I'll put his back out.)

"Good old Minna!" he cried. "Finding those keys! Fetching the rubbish bag! Letting me bury the dog among your petunias! We're fifty pounds richer today because of your help. Anything you want, Minna! Anything! Just name it!"

I thought. There's lots of things I want. But one thing I wanted more than anything else.

"Anything, Crusher?"

"Anything!"

"Anything at all?"

He was adamant.

"Anything you want."

"Right then," I said. "I want you to clean up that little pile of dog mess, straight away."

Crusher's all right. He went pale, and he didn't look at all pleased. But he went and did it. Straight away.

(And all you softies can come back now. It's all over.)

4
YOU DON'T LOOK
VERY POORLY

You don't exactly *ask* to get sick, do you? I mean, you don't go round *inviting* germs and viruses to move in and do their worst to your body. You don't actually *apply* for trembling legs and feeling shivery, and a head that's had a miniature steel band practising for a carnival in it all night.

And if you should happen to mention to your own mother that you feel absolutely terrible, you would expect a bit of sympathy, wouldn't you?

I wouldn't. Not any more.

"You don't *look* very poorly."

That's what she said. And she said it suspiciously, too, as if I was one of those people who's always making excuses to stay off school and spend the day wrapped in a downie on the sofa watching Bagpuss and Playschool and Pebble Mill at One.

"Well, I feel absolutely rotten."

"You don't look it."

"I'm sorry!" I snapped. (I was getting pretty cross.) "Sorry I can't manage a bright-green face for you! Or purple spots on my belly! Or all my hair falling out! But I feel rotten just the same!"

And I burst into tears.

(Now that's not like me.)

"Now that's not like you," said Mum, sounding sympathetic at last. "You must be a little bit off today."

"I am not *off*," I snarled through my tears. "I'm not leftover milk. Or rotten fish."

"There, there," Mum soothed. "Don't fret, Minna. Don't get upset. You just hop straight back up those stairs like a good poppet, and in a minute I'll bring something nice up on a tray, and you can have a quiet day in bed with Mum looking after you until you feel better."

That was a bit more like it, as I think you'll agree. So I stopped snivelling and went back to bed. I didn't exactly hop straight back up those stairs because I was feeling so crummy and weak I could barely drag myself up hanging on to the bannisters; but I got up somehow, and put on my dressing-gown and buttoned it right up to the top to keep my chest warm, and plumped up my pillows so I could sit comfortably, and switched on my little plastic frog reading-lamp, and folded my hands in my lap, and I waited.

And I waited.

And I waited.

44

(In case you're wondering, I was waiting for Mum to bring me up something nice on a tray and look after me until I felt better.)

She never came.

Oh, I'm sure that she *meant* to come. I'm sure she had every intention of coming. I'm sure it wasn't her fault the milkman came and needed paying, and it took time to work out what she owed because he'd been away for two weeks on his holiday in Torremolinos.

And I'm sure it wasn't Mum's fault that he took the opportunity to park his crate of bottles down on the doorstep and tell her all about the way some sneaky people always bagged the best pool-loungers by creeping down at dead of night and dropping their swimming towels over them; and how his wife's knees burned and peeled but none of the rest of her, even though all of her was out in the sun for the same amount of time; and how his daughter Meryl came home to her job at the Halifax with a broken heart because of some fellow called Miguel Angel Gippini Lopez de Rego, who danced like a fury but turned out to be engaged to a Spanish girl working in Barcelona.

Oh, it wasn't Mum's fault that she had to listen to all that before she could get away to bring me up something nice on a tray and look after me until I was better. But I could hear them talking clearly enough on the doorstep. And I don't actually recall hearing her say firmly but politely: "Excuse me, Mr Hooper, but Minna's in bed feeling terrible, and I must get back upstairs, so I'll listen to all the rest tomorrow." I heard quite a bit; but I didn't hear that.

As soon as the milkman had chinked off next

door, I thought I heard Mum making for the bottom of the stairs. But she never got there.

"YeeeeooooowwwwwwwaaaaaAAAAAAAAAAA-EEEEEEWWW!"

You guessed it. Crummy Dummy woke up.

And I suppose it wasn't Mum's fault that Crummy Dummy needed her nappy changing. And that there weren't any dry ones because we don't have a tumbler-drier and it had been raining for three solid days. And Crusher Maggot had forgotten to pick up a packet of disposable nappies before he went off to Sheffield for a few days to help the sister of a mate change flats.

So Mum decided the simplest thing would be to park Crummy Dummy in the playpen where little accidents don't matter. It wasn't her fault it took forever to drag it out of the cupboard because Crusher had dumped some great heavy lump of car innards right in front of it. Or that she had to fetch the damp nappies off the line and drape them over the rack in the kitchen.

And I suppose it's understandable that while she was shaking out the damp nappies, she should glance out of the window at the grey skies and think about nipping down to the launderette with the rest of the washing and handing it to Mrs Hajee to do in the machines, since it really didn't look as if it would ever stop raining.

So I suppose it does make sense that the very next thing I heard on my quiet day in bed was Mum bellowing up the stairs:

"Minna! *Minna*! Look after the baby for a few minutes, will you, while I nip down to the launderette? She's perfectly happy in her playpen with her toys. Just come down if she starts to squawk."

Fine. Lovely. Sure. Here am I, feeling really terrible and looking forward to something nice on a tray and being looked after until I feel better, and suddenly I'm looking after the baby! Fine. Lovely. Sure.

To be quite fair to Mum, she didn't stay out any longer than was absolutely necessary. There was the launderette, of course. And then she had to get the disposable nappies or Crummy Dummy would have had to spend the whole morning sitting on her cold bottom in the playpen, waiting for the ones in the kitchen to dry. And while she was in the supermarket she did pick up bread, and a quarter of sliced ham, and a few oranges and a couple of other things, making too many to get through the quick check-out. And there were really long queues at all the others because it was pension-day morning. And she did just pop into the newsagent's on her way home as well. And, yes, she did stop on the corner for a second, but that was just to be polite to the Lollipop Lady who told her that, whatever it was I'd got, there was a lot of it about, and Mum ought to be really careful or she'd come down with it as well.

And then she came straight home. She *says* she was out for no more than five minutes at the very most. But I've a watch, so I know better.

Then, at last, she came up to my room. She had Crummy Dummy tucked under one arm, all bare bottom and wriggles, and she was carrying a tray really high in the air, practically above her head, so Crummy Dummy couldn't upset it with all her flailing arms and legs. It was so high I couldn't see what was on it from the bed.

"I don't know how these nurses do it," said Mum. "They should have medals pinned on their chests, not watches."

I looked at mine. It was exactly half past ten. (I fell sick at 8.23.)

"If you were a nurse," I said, "you would have got the sack two hours ago."

"I'd like to see you do any better," she snapped back, sharpish.

"I bet I would," I told her. "I bet if *you* were sick, it wouldn't take *me* two whole hours to bring you something nice on a tray."

"I should wait till you see what there is on the tray before you start grumbling," Mum warned. And then she lowered it on to the bed in front of me.

And there was a cup of very milky coffee with bubbles on top in my favourite fat china bear mug, and a huge orange cut into the thinnest possible circular slices, just how I like it when I want to nibble at the peel as well. And a chocolate-biscuit bar and the latest *Beano* and *Dandy*, and a pack of twenty brand-new fine-tipped felt pens.

I felt dead guilty for being so grumpy.

"I'm sorry I said you'd get the sack as a nurse."

"Oh, that's all right," Mum answered cheerfully. She flipped Crummy Dummy over and put a nappy on her before there was trouble and even more laundry. "It's a well-known fact that it's even harder to be a good patient than a good nurse."

"Is that true?"

"Certainly."

And then, with Crummy Dummy safe at last, Mum sat down on my bed and took a break.

I thought about what she said quite a lot while I was getting better. As I sipped my coffee, and nibbled my orange circles, and read my *Beano*, and made my chocolate biscuit last as long as I could while I was drawing with my brand-new felt pens, I wondered what sort of patient Mum would make. She isn't famous in this house for longsuffering meekness or sunny patience.

And I wondered what sort of nurse I'd make – sensitive, deft, unflappable, efficient. . . .

I'd no idea I would find out so soon.

It was only two days later, on Saturday morning, that Mum leaned over the bannisters and called down:

"Minna, I feel just awful. Awful."

"You don't *look* very poorly."

(I didn't mean it that way. It just popped out.)

You'd have thought I was trying to suggest she was faking.

"I may not *look* it, but I *am*," she snapped. "I feel as

if I've been left out all night in the rain, and my bones have gone soggy, and hundreds of spiteful little men with steel boots are holding a stamping competition in my brain."

Personally, even without the Lollipop Lady saying there was a lot of it about, I would have recognized the symptoms at once.

I was determined to show Mum what proper nursing ought to be.

"You go straight back to bed," I ordered. "I'll take care of you, and everything else. You tuck yourself in comfortably, and I'll bring up something nice on a tray."

Mum swayed a little against the bannisters. She did look pale.

"You are an angel, Minna," she said faintly. And wrapping her shiny black skull-and-crossbones dressing gown more closely around her string-vest nightie, she staggered back into the bedroom.

I don't have to tell you about my plan, do I? You'll already have guessed. Yes, I was going to rush back into the kitchen and spread a tray with lovely, tempting treats for an invalid's breakfast – treats like a cup of tea made just the way Mum really likes it, golden-pale, not that thick, murky, dark sludge favoured by Crusher. (He says Mum's tea is too weak to crawl out of the pot.) And I was going to pick a tiny posy of flowers from my half of the garden, and arrange them in one of the pretty china egg cups.

And I was going to bring the tray up without delay.

Guess what went wrong first. No, don't bother. I'll tell you. First, I locked myself out. Honestly. Me,

Minna. The only one in the house who *never* does it. I did it. I was so keen to get my tray arranged that I stepped out of the back door into the garden to find the flowers without checking the latch.

Clunk!

The moment I heard the door close behind me, I realized. I could have kicked myself in the shins. I picked my way around to the front, just on the off-chance that the front door was unlocked. But I knew it wouldn't be, and of course it wasn't.

I stood there, thinking. I had two choices. I could ring the doorbell and drag poor, shaking, deathly-pale Mum from her bed of sickness and down the stairs to let me in; or I could slip next door to old Mrs Pitopoulos, ring her bell instead, and ask to borrow the spare key to our house she keeps for emergencies in an old cocoa tin under her sink.

I knew which a good nurse would do. I went next door and rang the bell.

No answer.

I rang again.

Still no answer.

Suddenly I noticed a faint scrabbling overhead. I looked up, and there was Mrs Pitopoulos in her quilted dressing-gown, fighting the stiff window-catch with her arthritic fingers.

She couldn't budge it, so she just beckoned me inside the house.

I tried the front door. It was locked. I went round the back, and that door opened. I picked my way

through the furry sea of all her pet cats rubbing their arched backs against my legs, so pleased to see me, and went upstairs.

Mrs Pitopoulos was sitting on the edge of her bed. Her face looked like a wrinkled sack, and her wig was all crooked.

"You look very poorly," I told her.

I couldn't help it. It just popped out.

"Oh, Minna," she said. "I feel terrible, terrible. My legs are rubber, and there are red-hot nails in my head."

"I've had that," I said. "Mum's got it now. The Lollipop Lady says that there's lots of it about."

When she heard this, Mrs Pitopoulos began to look distinctly better. Maybe when you're that age and you get sick, you think whatever it is has come to get you. At any rate, she tugged her wig round on her head, and even the wrinkles seemed to flatten out a bit.

"Minna," she said. "Would you do me a great favour, and feed my hungry cats?"

"What about you?" I said. "Have you had anything this morning?"

"Oh, I'm not hungry," Mrs Pitopoulos declared. But then she cocked her head on one side, and wondered about it. And then she added:

"Maybe I do feel just a little bit peckish. Yesterday my sister brought me all these lovely things: new-laid brown speckled eggs and home-made bread and a tiny pot of fresh strawberry jam. But what I'd really like is . . ." (Her eyes were gleaming, and she looked miles better.) "What I'd really like is a bowl of Heinz tomato soup with bits of white bread floating on the top."

Even I can cook that.

And so I did. And fed her cats. And she was so pleased when I brought the soup up to her on a tray that she pressed on me all the little gifts her sister had brought round the day before: the new-laid brown speckled eggs and home-made bread and tiny pot of fresh strawberry jam – oh, and the door key of course.

Mum was astonished when I brought the tray up. I thought she must have been asleep. She looked as if she had been dozing. She heaved herself upright against the pillows, and I laid the tray down on her knees.

"Minna!" she cried. "Oh, how lovely! Look at the flowers!"

You'd think someone who claims to like flowers so much would take a little bit more care with her half of the garden, wouldn't you?

"Wait till you've tasted the food," I said.

I could tell that she didn't really feel much like eating. But she was determined not to hurt my feelings, so she reached out and took one of the strips of hot buttered toast made from the home-made bread.

She nibbled the crust politely.

"Delicious," she said. And then, "Mmm. *Delicious.*"

She couldn't help dipping the next strip of toast into the new-laid brown speckled soft-boiled egg.

"Mmmm!" she cried. "This is *wonderful.*"

After the egg was eaten, she still had two strips of toast left. She spread one with the fresh strawberry jam, and off she went again.

"Mmmm! *Marvellous!*"

She went into raptures over the golden-pale tea. I

reckoned poor old Crusher would have a battle getting her back on the thick, murky, dark sludge when he came home. And then she leaned back against the pillows, smiling.

She looked a lot better.

"I'll bring you some more, if you'd like it," I offered.

"You are the *very best nurse*," Mum declared. "You managed all this, and so quickly too!"

Now I was sure she'd been dozing. I'd taken *ages*.

"You're the *very best patient*," I returned the compliment. "You don't notice what's going on, or how long it takes!"

"Silly," she said, and snuggled back under the bedcovers.

I think she must have thought I was joking.

5
CRUSHER MAGGOT'S
(STATELY) HOME

Early one Saturday morning, some old man we'd never even seen before came round to our house asking for Mr Pollard.

Mum answered the door in her nightie. (I wish she wouldn't.)

"*Who*?" she asked, slouching against the door frame.

"Mr Pollard," repeated the old man. "Mr Harold Pollard."

"I've never heard of him," Mum said. "He certainly doesn't live here."

"Sure?"

"Certain," said Mum.

"Pity." The old man shrugged. Lifting the carrier bag in his hand, he added: "Because this is definitely the address he wrote on the stub of the ticket that won this bottle of whisky in the pub raffle."

"Oh!" Mum clapped her hand over her mouth. "Harold Pollard! Of *course*! Yes, this is the right house."

She put out her hand to take the whisky. But the old man had turned away.

"Don't try that one on me!" he called back over his shoulder. "I might be old, but I'm not senile. It's only five seconds since you were telling me you'd never heard of Harold Pollard."

"I have, though," Mum insisted. "It's just that, for the moment, I completely forgot whose name it is."

But the old man was already halfway down the path, clutching the carrier bag to his chest and mumbling crossly to himself about the dishonesty of some people round here.

Mum turned on me. She was ratty.

"Now that's *your* fault!" She stamped her foot. "Who was it went and called him Crusher Maggot so often that I forgot his real name! I blame you for this, Minna!"

"He's your boyfriend, not mine," I defended myself. "You ought to remember his name. He'll blame *you*."

He did, too. He went pale as a maggot after he heard the terrible news, and went on all the rest of the morning about how he must have spent thousands of pounds on raffle tickets in his time, and never won so much as a stuffed furry monkey, and now that he'd finally won a whole bottle of whisky, Mum had as good as poured it down the sink.

And then, five minutes before opening time, he prised his winning raffle ticket out of his skin-tight leather cut-offs, and strode off down the pub in search of his prize.

He came back a little later in a slightly better temper, clutching the bottle of whisky.

"That old man hadn't had time to drink much of it," he told us. "Not more than a couple of swigs, anyhow."

I left the room. I was disgusted. Sometimes I think I am the only person in our household who actually believes in germs.

When I came back, Crusher was telling my mum off.

"You ought to be ashamed," he was saying, "not remembering the name of your own boyfriend. You ought to take a proper interest."

Mum scowled.

"I *do*." (I can't say that she sounded very convincing.)

"All right," Crusher Maggot challenged her. "I'll test you. How many brothers do I have?"

Mum wasn't sure.

"How many sisters?"

Mum wasn't sure about that, either.

"Where was I born?"

Mum knew the answer to that, of course, because he's got it tattooed on his head – MADE IN BIRMINGHAM. But then Crusher claimed that question didn't count, and asked another.

"Where was I brought up?"

Mum didn't know.

"See?" Crusher triumphed. "You really don't know the first thing about me!"

"Gran's always saying that," I reminded them both.

Neither looked pleased.

"All right!" Mum said. "You win. I don't know much about you. So instead of sitting there crowing about it, why don't you just tell me?"

"I'll go one better than that," claimed Crusher. "I'll *show* you."

And he went off to have a go at his new car.

"Where is he planning on taking us?" I asked.

"How should I know?" snapped Mum. "It's Crusher Maggot I know. Not Harold Pollard!"

I must say, I came to see what she meant as the day passed. We didn't go in Crusher's new car. It wouldn't start. So Crusher swung Crummy Dummy up on his shoulders, and we strolled up to our end of the bypass to catch a bus.

"Where are we going? Town or country?" I asked Crusher. (You can never tell which way people at the bus stop are heading since it's just before the roundabout.)

"Country," said Crusher. "Just outside a small village."

"Oh, ho!" cried Mum. "Pigpen Pollard, here we come!"

You could tell she was still in a really bad mood.

The bus took forever to turn up. And when it did, I wished it hadn't.

"Spindle Village, please," Crusher said to the driver.

The driver looked us up and down.

"Two seventies and one thirty-five," he said at last. "Babies are free."

Mum pointed at me.

"She's free, too," she said.

I was appalled. Simply appalled. I haven't been free on the buses for *years*.

While Crusher fed one pound forty into the ticket-machine, the driver peered at me above his spectacles.

"How old is she?" he asked suspiciously.

Even Mum couldn't bring herself to say "five". She just muttered something about me being rather big for my age, and poked me in the back. "Aren't you, Minna?"

"No," I said. "No, I'm not. I'm not at all big for my age. I'm quite normal. And children my age pay half on buses."

And I started to dig in my pockets for thirty-five pence.

"I'm going to let you off the fare," the driver said to me. "Because you're honest."

"Unlike some people," he added under his breath, as Mum moved past him down the bus.

(Good job it was practically empty, or I'd have died.)

All the way to Spindle, I questioned Crusher closely about the house he was brought up in.

"How many rooms does it have?"

"Two hundred and eight, not counting cellars."

"How many chimney pots?"

"Hundreds."

"How big is the garden?"

"What? In acres?"

I'm not quite sure about acres, so I said:

"Compared with that playground where Crummy Dummy likes the duck swings."

"Let me see . . ." Crusher was thinking. "About a hundred times bigger."

I grinned. I could keep going as long as he could.

"How far is it from the front gate to the front door?"

"About three-quarters of a mile."

I thought he was joking.

I thought he was joking until the bus stopped just before Spindle Village, and we got off outside the largest pair of wrought-iron gates I've ever seen in my life. They towered over me, and I'm no midget, I can tell you. Only my mother could look at me and still try to get me a free ride on a bus.

"Here we are."

"*Here?*"

"Yup."

"Is this *it?*"

"It certainly is."

"I don't *believe* you."

But Crusher couldn't have been kidding because he walked straight up to the stone wall that fringed the huge, high, curvy gates, and carefully prised a little slab of stone out from where it was sitting, neat and unnoticed, among all the others.

Behind it, hidden in the old wall, was a key. No one who hadn't known it was there could ever have found it.

"Come on, then," he said, unlocking the padlock that held the gates closed. "Let's go and meet my dad."

I must say I felt a bit nervous about meeting

Crusher's – sorry, Harold's – father if this was where he lived. I wished we could turn back and forget it. I didn't think we *looked* right. I thought that Crusher should have warned us earlier. Because Mum was wearing her sequinned bikini top with the gold tassels and her baggy pink-spotted bloomer trousers, and she had spent the boring bus ride brushing up Crummy Dummy's hair into fresh spikes. She looked just like a circus clown with a punk baby.

Mind you, Crusher looked just as outlandish with his enormous rainbow Mohican, and chains all over, and one of his black skin-tight leather trouser legs cut off a good half-metre above the other.

But he's not my mother, or my baby sister.

Crusher swung Crummy Dummy back on his shoulders, and we set off along the wooded drive. It was cool and dark, like an airy green tunnel, and so quiet you could hear the birds flap away as we walked round each lazy curve. The flickering specks of light between the trees grew larger and fiercer, till suddenly we stepped out on a stretch of road heaped high on either side with glorious red bushes.

"Rhododendrons," said Crusher.

I'm glad he told us. I was quite interested to see a rhododendron. Gran says she was always having to spell them at school.

And then, coming round the last bend, we saw the house. Mum and I stopped to stare. It was the most enormous mansion, with rows and rows and rows of windows, standing behind a huge green lawn. I've never seen a lawn that big before. Miles and miles of flat, unbroken green. And not a speck of litter. Not *one*. Our old headmaster would have burst into tears if he'd seen it.

We weren't alone, though. Standing right on the edge of the lawn was someone peering closely into a flowerbed. The sun sailed behind a sliver of cloud and he lifted his head. Spotting Crusher, who had moved out of the shadows, he suddenly started walking towards us.

He looked dead posh. I felt quite frightened. Mum did, too, I think. At least, she hung back out of sight with me, among the rhododendrons. But Crusher kept on striding forward with Crummy Dummy on his shoulders, getting closer and closer to the man who was walking towards him – to throw him out, I thought, until I heard him booming across the lawn:

"Good Lord! Is that young Harry Pollard? Fancy your rolling home like this, out of the blue!" The man stopped and took a proper look at Crusher. "Still stamping around looking like an Apache, I see."

Gran says the same. Quite often. But whereas Gran says it rather rudely, I always think, this man clearly didn't mean a thing by it. He was just being friendly.

"Fine baby you've got there, Harry," he added admiringly, as he came close. "Chip off the old block?"

Crusher gave him a big wide grin, and let go of one of Crummy Dummy's ankles to wave a hand about expansively.

Crummy Dummy toppled sideways.

I rushed out of the shadows. (To do her credit, so did Mum.)

The posh man stared. He did try not to, you could tell. But he just couldn't help it. Perhaps he was used to young Harry Pollard turning up looking like an Apache. He could even handle one little, look-alike Apache baby. But he couldn't quite manage Mum, with her sequinned bikini top with gold tassels and her baggy pink-spotted bloomer trousers.

He swallowed a bit.

Then,

"How do you do, Madam?" he asked Mum, offering her his hand to shake. "A lovely day. Most

clement. Mmm?" (He seemed to want to get safely on to the weather, I thought.)

"Smashing," said Mum. "No rain at all."

The man shook his head sadly.

"A poor look-out for the crops, though. . . ."

Mum stared. She's got no sympathy for farmers, my mum. Like Gran, she reckons they all make sure they do all right for themselves. Whenever the newsreaders on the telly look serious and mention the farmers, my mum's lips curl and she sings the chorus to that song,

'Oi've never seen a farmer on a boike;

No, Oi've never seen a farmer on a boike. . . .'

She didn't even hum it this time, though. She just kept quiet.

Then the man noticed me, hiding behind Mum. He held out his hand. I wiped mine, and shook it.

"And this young lady."

I took a deep breath.

"Your rhododendrons are quite lovely," I told him.

"Thank you," he replied. "Thank you so much. I *am* rather proud of my rhododendrons."

And then, you could just tell, he'd had enough of us, and wanted to get back to his flowerbeds. His eyes glazed over.

"I'll let you all get on now, shall I?" he murmured. Then, turning to Crusher: "You don't happen to be going along by the greenhouses, do you, Harry?"

"We-ell . . ." Crusher looked doubtful. "I *was* just going to pop inside and see my dad."

"Of course! Of course!" The man tried not to look too disappointed. "Naturally. So you'd better go straight in by the front."

"Righty-ho," Crusher said. "Sir."

(I've only ever heard Crusher say "Sir" once before, and that was to the policeman who stopped him after his exhaust pipe fell off, and was wondering whether to bother to charge him.)

"Lovely to see you," the man said. "Mustn't leave it so long next time."

He smiled politely and shook hands with everyone all over again – even with Crummy Dummy on top of Crusher's shoulders. She chortled away when he reached up and shook her fingers. She was delighted.

"He was nice," Mum said as we traipsed over the lawn towards the mansion. "Who was he, then?"

"Lord Harbinger," said Crusher. "He's all right, he is. Not a bad stick."

Mum fell silent at that. She was thinking. So was I. If she was thinking what I was thinking, it was this: if Crusher's home was so incredibly posh that even the man who looked after the flowerbeds had a title, then who might we meet behind the front door? Viscount Pollard? The Marquis of Spindle? Even King Harold? Maybe my mum's boyfriend was actually a Prince in Disguise. It didn't seem likely. (I peered at Crusher Maggot sideways: no, it didn't seem likely.) But you never know . . . And if his dad lived in this house . . .

You've never seen a front door like it. I bet you they nicked it off a cathedral. It was so large it had whole doors set into it, in case you couldn't be bothered to open the entire thing. It was so enormous it made me feel small enough to go free on the buses.

But Crusher just waltzed straight on up to it as

though it were any old front door, and laid his hand
on one of the great brass bell pulls.

Mum got even more nervous.

"Are you sure this is right?" she asked, reaching
up to lift Crummy Dummy off Crusher's shoulders.

"I lived here, didn't I?" Crusher said haughtily. "I
ought to *know*."

And he tugged at the great brass bell pull.

From deep inside the mansion, we heard the low,
throaty jangle of a far-off, echoing bell. I'm sorry to
turn all poetic, but that's the sort of noise it was.

A minute passed. And then another. I thought I
could hear footsteps, but I was just imagining it. I
got more and more apprehensive. And so did Mum.
But Crusher just stood there muttering about not
having all day, and the time of the last bus home,
and his father pretending he had rheumatism.

Suddenly I did hear something. A heavy, grinding
noise, like someone pulling back a rusty bolt. And
then metallic clinks and rattlings, as if a huge key
were being pushed inside a lock, and turned. Then a
creak. Then a squeaking.

And then there was a sudden rush of cold air, and,
standing in front of us blinking at the daylight he
had let in on himself was a man in a black uniform
with gold braid on his sleeves, and gold buttons, and
a black cap with gold along its peak.

"Harold!" the man cried.

"Dad!" shouted Crusher.

They fell into each other's arms. They hugged
each other. They patted one another's backs. They
stroked each other's hair. They clapped one another
on the shoulders.

"What a surprise!"

"Good to see you, Dad."

"You should have *said*."

"Spur of the moment, Dad."

"I could have bought *cake*!"

Then the old man noticed the rest of us.

First he saw Mum, so he stopped patting Crusher.

"Pleased to meet you," he told her, though he looked just a little bit doubtful.

Mum smiled. I think she was simply glad that Crusher's dad hadn't turned out to be even posher than Lord Harbinger. But it came out as one of her radiant, winning, sunshine smiles (the kind she turns on our headmaster when she's missed four PTA meetings in a row) and Crusher's dad was lost at once.

Then he saw Crummy Dummy, and tears welled in his eyes. (You could tell straight away he was one of those grandpa-style softies.)

"Is this your baby, lad?" he asked. His voice choked up so fast he could barely speak.

"Sort of," said Crusher.

The old man reached out. Crummy Dummy's not so daft. She knows when she is on to a good thing. Squealing with joy, she threw herself into his arms. She likes older people. They remind her of Gran.

The old man patted her on her wet nappy, and turned to me.

"And this young lady?" he enquired.

"This is Minna," said Crusher. "She tries to keep me and her mum in order."

"I'm pleased to meet you," Crusher's father said. "And certainly in respect of Harold here, I hope your efforts are crowned with more conspicuous success than my own."

"What?" Crusher said, all suspicious.

I got it, though.

We all trooped through the door. Along one corridor, and then another. Round a few corners. Down a passage or two. Through the odd half-open doorway, I caught quick glimpses of the most fabulous rooms, rich with rhododendron-coloured drapes and patterned rugs, all chock-a-block with polished tables and precious china and bowls of flowers. Then we followed Crusher's father down a short flight of steps, and then another. Along one more corridor, round one last corner, and into Crusher's dad's part of the mansion. (No wonder it took him so long to answer the door.)

There wasn't anything worth having for tea. And even if there had been, I bet he wouldn't have been able to find it. He seemed in a real dither, what with making sure everyone had a comfortable chair, and checking he'd got all our names off pat, and telling Mum and me about his job.

"Oh yes," he claimed over his cup of tea. "It's a very good position. Doorman to Lord Harbinger. It's suited me for twenty-five years. It'll suit me until I turn up my toes."

But we couldn't stay that long. Crusher kept saying we ought to be making our way back to the bus stop, or we'd be stranded overnight.

Mr Pollard turned all wistful when he realized we were really going, and taking Crummy Dummy with us. Those two had really taken a shine to one another. She'd spent the afternoon on his lap, practically purring, while he made a point of referring to her as "Miranda", and brushing her hair spikes down with the palm of his hand.

"You must come and see us," Mum consoled him at the door. "You're Crusher's family, so you're always welcome."

"Right." Crusher tried to tempt his dad. "I won a bottle of whisky in a raffle today. You come and visit us, and we'll drink it."

And Crummy Dummy blew him a lovely, farewell bubble.

We walked back over the wide, green lawns. Lord Harbinger nodded at us politely as we passed by the flowerbed. He gave a special wave to Crummy Dummy, and looked quite disappointed to see her hair all soft and flat.

Mum coughed up my half fare on the bus without arguing. I was glad about that. It had been a long day.

6
"ALL RIGHT"

Meeting Crusher's old father that day set me off
wondering about my own dad. It's not as if I've ever
seen that much of him. In fact, there were times I
could barely recall what he looked like. I knew
he worked in a big garage about a hundred and
fifty miles down the motorway, but whenever I
asked Mum anything more about him, she only
said:

"Oh, he's all right."

It isn't much to build on, is it?

"Well, is he *good-looking*?"

"He looks all right."

"Is he *intelligent*?"

"His brain works all right."

"Is he *amusing*?"

"He made me laugh all right, I suppose."

"Is he *kind*?"

"He was always all right with me and the cats."

I lost my temper then.

"If he was never any better than *all right*," I
snapped, "why did you bother to have *me*?"

Mum laughed, and stretched out her hand to
stroke my hair.

"Oh, *you*," she said. "You're all right, too, you are."

You see? Hopeless. Absolutely hopeless. So I gave up.

But then, a few days later in school, we started something new: a project on Families. Mr Russell told everyone to be quiet, and then he tossed up to see whether we were to start with mothers or fathers. And fathers won, so fathers it was.

"I haven't got one," Andrew said.

"Neither have I."

"Mine's in Australia."

"Lucky you!"

Then Mr Russell told everyone to be quiet again.

"If you haven't got your own, real, original, biological father," he said, "pick out the person who comes closest. Pick someone –" He paused, and waved his hands around in the air, searching for an example. "Pick someone you would ask to fix your bike."

"I haven't got a bike," said Joel.

"My mum always fixes my bike," said Sarah.

"I *asked* my dad to fix my bike," grumbled Arif. "Six weeks ago! He hasn't even *looked* at it yet." He scowled, and added with real bitterness: "*And* he's my own, real, original, biological dad."

"My uncle fixes my bike. He's got a bike shop."

"Nothing has ever gone wrong with my bike."

"I've never even had a bike," Joel said sadly.

"At least you've got a father," said Andrew.

Joel was just telling us he thought he'd much prefer a bike, when Mr Russell told everyone to be quiet again.

"Father," he said. "Or someone like it. I want a

picture or a photograph, and two whole sides of writing, by Friday."

We all groaned loudly. And by the time Mr Russell had told everyone to be quiet again, the bell had rung.

I ran off home.

Mum was leaning against the draining-board. She was wearing her plum-coloured plastic boots and her fishnet stockings. She was fiddling with her tarantula earrings. Crusher Maggot was slouching at the kitchen table, wearing funny dark glasses and playing a tune on his skull with his knuckles.

What do they *do* all day long when I'm away at school, that's what I'd like to know.

I asked Mum:

"Do you have a photo of my real dad?"

"Yes," she said. "No. I don't know. No. Yes."

I do try to be very patient.

"Which?" I said. "Yes or no?"

"Both, really," she replied. "I do have a photo of him, yes. But I'm afraid that my left elbow got in front of most of his face, and what little of him is showing is terribly blurry. You'd never know that it was him."

"Weren't there any other photos?"

Mum tipped her head on one side to think. One of the tarantula earrings crawled over her cheek, and the other got tangled in her hair. It was very off-putting.

"There were some others," she recalled. "But you were in them, too, so he took those with him."

I thought that was a little daft, myself. One of them might have realized I would grow up, and want to see them. But, still as patient as could be, I asked:

"Where is this famous photo of part of his blurred face and your left elbow?"

"I'm not sure," Mum said. "I think I've lost it."

(I simply can't *think* why they call it "home" work. I'd stand a better chance of getting it done on the *moon*.)

"I need a photo," I told her, "to take to school."

"Take that nice one of Crusher," she told me.

I've mentioned this photograph of Crusher before, I think. Do you remember? It's the one with his hair in flaming red and orange spikes, and his teeth ferociously bared, and his tattoo showing.

"No, thank you," I answered as politely as possible. "I'd like one of my own, real, original, biological father."

"All right," said Crusher. "Suit yourself. I'll ask him for one next time I see him."

I turned and stared.

"*See* him?" I said. "Do you get to see him?"

"Quite often," Crusher said. "I always fill up with petrol at his garage. Why, I stopped in and had a couple of words with him only a week ago."

I was amazed. Simply amazed.

"How is he?" I asked. "How is my very own, real, original, biological father?"

Crusher wasn't at all irritated by this display of crippling sarcasm.

"All right," he said. "He was all right."

But Mum was a little put out by my rudeness.

"Original and biological he may be," she said. "But who fixes your bike?"

(I'd really like to know where they pick up all this fix-your-bike business.)

I was still angry.

"Next time," I said, as cold as ice, "next time that someone drops in to have a few words with my own, real, original, biological father, do you think they might possibly bother to mention it to me?"

"I'll do better than that," Crusher offered. "I'll take you down there."

"When?"

"When you like."

I thought about it.

"I need the photo before Friday," I told him.

"Tomorrow, then."

"*All right*," I said. "Tomorrow. *All right*."

So that's how it came about that the very next day I borrowed next door's fancy new camera, and Crusher borrowed the other side's car since his own still wasn't going, and I travelled with him all the way down the motorway. It meant I had to take the whole afternoon off school. Mum said it didn't matter since I'd be doing school work in taking the photo, but I didn't dare tell that one to Mr Russell. That sort of thinking really annoys him. He calls it "slack". I did consider trying to explain, but he was in one of his terribly busy moods and in the end I just did what everyone else in the class does, and told him that I had to go to the dentist.

It took Crusher and me exactly two hours and forty minutes to drive down the motorway as far as the garage.

It was a big one, set back a little from the road. There were several lines of pumps, and every one of them was busy with people filling cars and motorbikes.

Crusher pulled up beside the air and water.

"Tell you what," he suggested, picking next door's fancy new camera off the back seat and thrusting it into my hands. "I'll give you over to your own, real, original, biological dad, and then I'll nip off for a while and do what I was going to do."

"What *were* you going to do?" I asked, suddenly suspicious.

First Crusher looked blank, then a little bit shifty.

"I really haven't the time to stop and explain," he told me.

I gave him a look – one of my *searching* looks.

"You drove all the way down here just to bring me to see my dad, didn't you?" I accused him.

"No, I didn't," said Crusher.

"Oh yes you did."

"No, I didn't."

"You did. I can tell."

"All right," said Crusher, embarrassed. "*All right*. Maybe I did, but I certainly didn't drive all this way just to sit in the front seat of the car arguing with you."

And he got out.

I followed. Crusher was looking round the garage forecourt. Suddenly he nudged my elbow.

"There," he said, nodding towards a man in overalls who was bending over a pile of cut-price tyres. "There he is."

"Really?"

"Yes. That's him."

And Crusher bellowed across the crowded fore-court:

"Hey, Bill! *Bill*! Here's your young Minna come to see you!"

The man in overalls lifted his head and stared in our direction. I say "our" direction, but it was only "my" direction by then, because Crusher Maggot had disappeared in a flash after making his an-nouncement, and I was left standing alone on the petrol-station forecourt, clutching a camera, and ten yards from my own, real, original, biological father I hadn't seen for ages.

It was all right. In fact, he was jolly nice, really. He gave me tons of comics and free bars of chocolate from the garage shop, and a brand-new film for the people next door to make up for my borrowing their camera. He helped me take a lot of photos, and even showed me how to set the time-release button so we could get some of us standing together with his arm round my shoulders. He made me promise to send him copies of all the ones that came out properly, and he laughed like a drain when I told him about the only photo of him that Mum has left.

He asked quite a lot of questions about our family, and he seemed pretty interested when I told him all about Crummy Dummy. He said he was glad to hear I had company now, and he made me promise to send a photo of her, too. And a good one of Mum.

He asked me about school, and my friends, and the house. He said that he was very pleased to hear I could swim, and he sounded interested in my roller-skating. Then he left someone else looking after the forecourt, and took me for a spin up the motorway in one of the open sports cars parked round the back of the garage.

That was fantastic. The wind blew my hair till it stuck out like Mum's. (He said I looked a bit like Mum, anyway.) He drove miles faster than Crusher Maggot does, and when I told him so, he grinned, and said that he was glad to hear it.

I didn't know quite what to call him. I tried to say the word "Dad" once or twice, but it sort of got stuck because I didn't know him well enough yet. Then he said: "Why don't you just call me Bill? Everyone else does." And that was easier.

When we drove back towards the garage, I could see Crusher standing, waiting, on the forecourt.

Bill slowed the car right down. And just before we came close enough for Crusher to overhear, he asked me privately:

"Do you get on with him? Is he all right?"

I looked at Crusher, who was watching me anxiously to see how I was getting on with my own, real, original, biological father.

"Yes," I said. "He's all right."

"Good," Bill said. "Good."

So that was that, really. The three of us shared a quick cup of tea out of the machine, and I ate one more chocolate bar, and took one more for the journey. Bill insisted on filling the car up for nothing. "It's not every day my daughter comes down to visit me," he said. Then Crusher and I got in and drove off.

I waved, and Bill waved and shouted that he'd pop in next time he came up our way, and I was to give his best wishes to Mum. Then we were out of sight.

Crusher settled himself more comfortably in the seat, then:

"Well?"

"All right," I told him. "He was all right."

When we got home, it was dark. Mum was really pleased to see us. All of the photos came out fine. Some were really good. (I've got the best ones pinned on my bedroom wall now.) I even managed the two whole pages of writing about my own, real, original, biological father – though I could tell that Mr Russell was really disappointed that I'd chosen to do him instead of Crusher Maggot, whom he's seen hanging around for me at the school gates.

And now, as you can see, I'm in the habit too. Yesterday, when Arif and I were sitting on the curbside watching poor Crusher trying to fix our

bikes, Arif asked me what my real father was like. And, without even thinking, I answered:

"Oh, he's all right."

Sometimes I worry that I'm getting just like all the rest of them, honestly I do.

7
ELK MONEY

I've never been in trouble at school before. And, mind you, even this time it wasn't really my fault. It was my mum's.

I may have mentioned to you before that, when it comes to getting me to school every day, and on time, my mum could do better. It's really up to me. If I didn't watch out for myself, I'd never get through the gates in the morning before the bell rings and, if I did, I'd have the world's worst bags under my eyes.

You're going to find it a little hard to believe, but this is how bedtime generally goes in our house:

ME: I really think I ought to be going up to bed now.
MUM: (*astonished*) Why?
ME: (*patiently*) Because it's getting rather late.
MUM: It's not *that* late.
ME: (*looking at my watch*) It's well past my bedtime.
MUM: Oh, you're getting older all the time. You don't need that much sleep.

ME: I do. Look at me. I've already got great big grey bags under my eyes.

MUM: That's just the light.

ME: No, it isn't.

MUM: Well, what about this board game? Surely you can stay up just long enough to finish the *game*? It's nearly over.

ME: It's nowhere near over. It'll take *ages*.

MUM: (*sulking*) Oh, well. Suit yourself . . .

ME: (*firmly*) Mum, I need my sleep!

MUM: Oh, all *right*. Go on, then. I'll come up in a little while and tuck you in.

ME: (*really relieved*) Oh, good, Mum. Thanks.

See? It's ridiculous. It's the same battle every single night. I just can't stand it. And often I turn up at school the next morning, yawning, with real grey-blue shadows under my eyes. And don't think Mr Russell doesn't notice.

Then, one day, I was really late. And that wasn't my fault, either. It was Mum's.

It happened on Tuesday. Tuesday's the day we're all supposed to bring in our Elk Money. It isn't much. It's only ten pence each, but it's important because our class is sponsoring this elk. All the schools in our district were sent these letters from the local zoo, begging for sponsors. Mr Russell is very democratic by nature, so our class got to vote for what we wanted. We argued for weeks, and in the end we voted to ask for a gorilla. But we had taken so long discussing the matter democratically that elks were all the zoo had left by then. Miss MacPherson across the corridor isn't a bit democratic by nature. She just chose any old animal herself, and wrote back the same day. She chose the gorilla and her class got it. Henry Boot overheard Mr Russell muttering something in the corridor about "simple dictatorship being a very easy matter", but Miss MacPherson snapped back at him pretty sharpish about "the limits of democracy", and was cross enough not to share her gorilla.

So our class has this elk. Her name is Elsie and she eats a lot. "Keep those ten pences rolling into school," pleads Mr Russell. I think he worries that if enough of us forget to shell out, then he will have to make up the amount himself. We all know exactly how poor he is, because they're always telling you about teachers' pay on the telly. So we all try very hard to remember our Elk Money every Tuesday, and Mr Russell gets quite testy if we forget.

And I forgot. Well, I didn't *forget*. I remembered

only too well. It was just that I hadn't any money of
my own, and Mum refused to lend me any of hers.
It's not that she's mean. She's not. In fact, Gran says
she's positively *daft* with her money. It's just that

she disapproves of zoos. Hates them, in fact. She says the animals are cramped and miserable and bored silly, and now almost everyone's got a colour telly there's no excuse for zoos at all, and she won't support them.

"I'm not asking you to build a new east wing for the monkeys," I said. "I just want to borrow ten pence Elk Money off you. That's *all*. Ten pence isn't going to keep the zoo gates open, is it?"

"I'm sorry," said Mum. "I really am. But you know how I feel about zoos. So I *can't* lend you your Elk Money."

"But, Mum! If I haven't got ten pence, I'll be in trouble!"

"I'm sorry, Minna. But the answer's *no*."

I must say, I was pretty shocked. Wouldn't you be? Your very own flesh and blood prepared to drop you in the soup like that, rather than lend a miserable old ten pence!

Extraordinary!

In fact, *so* extraordinary that I thought about it all the way to school that morning. I couldn't help it. I was trying to work out just what it was about the lives of animals in zoos that so offended her.

And maybe I did drift off into a bit of a daydream about what it really would feel like to be a gorgeous, powerful, wild tiger locked up for ever in a small pen and yard no larger than somebody's back garden. And maybe I did make-believe a little that I was a baby chimpanzee, chock-full of beans, and couldn't ever swing any higher or wider than the top of the cage or the sides of the cage. Maybe I did get thinking really deeply, and slow down walk- ing, and start to drag my feet a bit along the paving-stones, and take my time, wondering, wondering . . .

I didn't know I was going to be *that* late, did I? And there was absolutely no need at all for Mr Russell to say in quite so waspish a tone of voice:

"I've had quite enough of this, Minna! Last week you said you had a dental appointment and disappeared for the entire afternoon. On Monday you turned up so tired I could see the bags under your eyes. Today you're horribly late and, on top of everything, you've even forgotten to bring in your Elk Money! Now I'm going to send a note home with you today, asking your mother to come in to school tomorrow morning and have a little chat about things."

My eyes must have gone as round as saucers. I simply couldn't think what good he thought talking to my Crummy Mummy would do!

But there's no accounting for teachers, so I just kept quiet.

I did try to get Mum to dress sensibly for the meeting, though.

"*Not* the angora top with the puff sleeves and the low bosom," I told her. "And *not* the purple, scalloped wellies. *Not* the plastic viper necklace. And *no* yellow eye-shadow. *Please*, Mum."

Mum put her head inside a Tesco paper bag.

"I suppose you'd like me to go in to school like this," she said.

"That's nice," said Crusher Maggot. "That really suits you."

I sighed. At times it's like living with two small children, honestly it is.

I did what I could. I hid some of the worst of her clothes and jewellery, and set my alarm clock for half an hour earlier the following morning. As soon as I was dressed, I went and stood in the doorway watching her sternly while she chose her clothes. She knew I meant business. She saw the steely look in my eyes. She didn't argue. When we walked into school, she looked practically normal.

"Right," I warned her between gritted teeth. "Whatever he says, *whatever*, nod and agree! Promise?"

"Promise," said Mum. (Credit where credit's due, she does mean well.)

Mr Russell clearly thought so, anyhow. He was quite taken with her. They spent a lot of time together, laughing and chatting outside the staff-room door. I peeped down the corridor twice, and both times Mum was obediently nodding. Mr Russell was so bewitched he even handed her his morning cup of coffee, the one he says he needs so badly he'd have to prop his eyelids apart with matchsticks if he didn't get it. And when he finally came back, alone, into the classroom, he leaned over my desk and whispered in my ear.

"*What* a nice Mum you have, Minna! Very cooperative. She's so prepared to be helpful that when I asked if she'd come on the Friday field trip to the zoo to see Elsie our elk, she nodded and agreed."

I buried my head in my hands. I could have *wept*.

We had a blazing row about it when I got home.

"Why did you say that?" I shouted at her. "Why did you say you would come with us to the zoo on Friday? You know you won't. You can't *bear* zoos. So you know you can't go. When Mr Russell invited you on the trip, why did you simply *nod and agree*?"

"But that's exactly what you *told* me to do, Minna!" she retorted. "That's what you made me promise! *Nod and agree!*"

"But not to go to the zoo!"

"*Whatever*, you said. Whatever he says, nod and agree!"

Sometimes I feel like despairing, truly I do.

"But what on earth will we do when Friday comes?"

"We'll think of something between us."

"Well, let's think *now*."

So we all sat there, thinking. And it was Crusher who came up trumps. He said to Mum:

"Why don't you send Gran along in your place? She likes zoos a lot. She can tell Mr Russell that Crummy Dummy kept sneezing, so you thought you should keep her at home, and she has come to help instead."

I know a good idea when I hear it.

"Brilliant!" I enthused. Gran is great fun. She'd

make any visit to a zoo a treat, and everyone in my class would like her.

"Brilliant!" Mum agreed. She was relieved. She hadn't wanted to let anyone down.

"Brilliant!" echoed Crusher. (He's never been overburdened with modesty, our Crusher.)

And I was satisfied.

But only for a while. For inexplicably, behind my back, without noticing, the most peculiar thing began to happen.

I went off zoos. Honestly. Just like that. Maybe it started with all that wondering I did on the way to school that morning, I don't know, but one day I was as happy to go and see Elsie our elk as the next person in the class and, on the next, you wouldn't have prised me through the zoo gates with a crowbar. I just knew the mere sight of all those miserable, penned-up bears and lions and apes would make me sick, and after the end of term when we'd be giving up the Elk Money anyway, not one penny of mine would ever find its way inside a zoo again.

"But what shall I do tomorrow?" I wailed at Mum. "I've been in so much trouble in school already! And if I can't go to the zoo with everyone else, what am I going to say to Mr Russell?"

We all thought again. And, once again, it was Crusher who came up with the answer.

"Minna," he said. "Here's twenty pence. Go down to the shop, will you, and fetch my newspaper, please? It's pretty chilly outside, so don't wrap up well."

I'm not an idiot. I got the message.

"Brilliant!" I enthused.

"Brilliant!" Mum agreed.

"Brilliant!" echoed Crusher.

I took Crummy Dummy with me in the pushchair. I wrapped her up warmly, but left my own coat off. I even wore my leaky wellingtons. I traipsed through every puddle I could find, and dawdled on every windy street corner.

When I got home, it was already supper-time. Crusher had cooked instant curry and tapioca pudding. He knows I won't eat either.

"Minna's completely lost her appetite," said Crusher, staring at my untouched plate. "Perhaps she's about to come down with a chill."

"Maybe," said Mum. She was fiddling with the pepper-pot lid. "She looks quite peaky."

She made a sudden movement and the lid sprang off the pepper-pot. Pepper flew out in clouds. Before I could blink, both Mum and Crusher had stuffed wads of paper tissue against their noses and mouths. They must have been keeping them ready, under the table.

Crummy Dummy and I sneezed. We sneezed and sneezed. We couldn't help it. Pepper was everywhere.

"Dear me!" cried Mum, her voice reeking with false innocence. "Minna and Crummy Dummy must have come down quite suddenly with shocking colds."

"So they must," Crusher agreed with her. "What a shame. It looks as if they both will have to stay home tomorrow."

"Oh, certainly," said Mum. "No question about it. No zoo trip for Minna, I'm afraid. Why, she might develop pneumonia! I'll just have to ask Gran if she minds going on the trip with the class by herself."

(At moments like this, I don't know why I call her Crummy Mummy. She always comes up trumps when I really need her. I can cope pretty well with most things. But it is good to have someone on your side when you feel really stumped. And she's on my side.)

So. Friday came, and I missed all of it. Mum kept me in. She was dead firm. She even made Crusher Maggot fetch his own paper. We sat together most of the day, playing cards, while Crummy Dummy bounced up and down in her cot, or crawled around the floor stuffing bits of carpet fluff into her earholes. I wore my rabbit slippers and two extra woollies in case Mr Russell sent spies round on their way home from school to check that I was ill. (Yes, honestly. He really does do that.)

But Gran was our only visitor. She turned up shortly after four, pink-cheeked and radiant! She'd had a *lovely* time, she told us. She'd *thoroughly* enjoyed the bus ride. She *loved* the zoo – so well laid out, with all those pretty little white signposts! Elsie the Elk was a *poppet*, and, as for that Mr Russell, he was *sweet*. (He was so sorry to hear about the colds. He hoped poor little Minna wasn't too disappointed at missing the zoo trip, and that little baby Miranda would soon be well enough for Mum to be able to get about again). All of the children, Gran said, were helpful and charming, and a *very* nice little boy called Henry Boot had carried her umbrella for her the whole afternoon. You couldn't have *faulted* the weather, and the candy floss tasted as heavenly as it did when she was a child herself. The zoo-keepers **were** friendly and pleasant, and all of the animals looked *thoroughly well looked after*, she must say. She'd had a *splendid* day, oh yes, *splendid*.

And how was I?

I gave the tiniest little cough.

"Oh, dear!" she cried, and fell all over me, cuddling and fussing. You'd have thought that I really and truly did have pneumonia. (She's a good Gran. Like Mum and Crusher, she comes up trumps.)

So that was it. Of course, I heard the other side of the story as soon as I went back to school on Monday morning. I hadn't missed much, everyone said. They weren't allowed to climb on the railings, and they weren't allowed to buy chips or ice-cream, and half of the animals were lying, fast asleep, at the back of their cages, and those that were outside and on their feet were pretty boring really, not doing anything like you see on the telly. And Elsie the Elk looked as if she had mange, and the candy floss had gone up to forty-five pence for a mean little stickful, and the bus ride was rotten because the driver wouldn't let them open the windows all the way, or sing at all loudly. And the only really good bit in the whole day, everyone said, was when Henry Boot threw up outside the wombat's cage. In case you're wondering, it wasn't any sudden, delicate sensitivity to the poor wombat's plight that made him sick, it was far too much chocolate.

Well. There you are. As my gran's very fond of saying, there's more than one way to tell any story. I've done my best with all these, though. I hope you liked them.

Minna

Also by Anne Fine

GOGGLE-EYES

'When it comes to a story, I just tell 'em better.'

Kitty Killin is not only a good story-teller but also the World's Great Expert when it comes to mothers having new and unwanted boyfriends, particularly when there's the danger they might turn into new and unwanted stepfathers.

Funny, touching, with Anne Fine's distinctive blend of humour and realism, this is an irresistible tale.

'*Goggle-Eyes* is a winner: witty, sensitive and warmhearted . . . a lovely book' – *Guardian*

A PACK OF LIARS

'You can't write lies,' repeated Oliver. 'You can't just write *a pack of lies!*'

Why is it that all the penpals Laura and Oliver get are either so boring they send you to sleep, or complete basket cases? For Laura, tedious Miranda is the last straw. So, taking on the identity of the imaginary Lady Melody Estelle Priscilla Hermione Irwin, Laura begins an extraordinary correspondence with the unsuspecting Miranda and weaves a fantastic tissue of lies about herself and her exotic life. But Laura soon learns she's not the only one capable of successful deception . . .

Fast and funny, sharp and perceptive, this is a captivating story by a first-class writer.

'As entertainment it rates highly' – *Junior Bookshelf*

THE BOOK OF THE BANSHEE

Friday 29th September. 07.52 hours. *Dawn Attack!*

Will Flowers is living in a war zone and the biggest explosions of all are coming from Estelle, his teenage sister. Will's parents start making battle plans, his sister, Muffy, no longer speaks and Will has taken to reading a First World War journal for comfort. But when his favourite author comes to school and tells them 'You can write about *anything,*' Will takes up the challenge. He becomes an Impeccable War Reporter – treading carefully between the warring factions. But soon he finds himself having to choose whether to remain impartial, or join the war in the hope for peace.

'A humorous, fast-moving, yet thoughtful book' – *School Librarian*

'Anne Fine's hilariously acute observations of verbal sparring will be familiar to all those similarly afflicted' – *Scotsman*

ROUND BEHIND THE ICE-HOUSE

Tom wants to forget – to get back into the past when he and Cass were still so close. What are the secrets she is keeping from him? Tom has to face the fact that as he and Cass grow up, they have to grow apart. He may be her twin brother but he doesn't own her and he never can.

A powerful and unusual story about the tensions of changing relationships.

FIGHTING IN BREAK AND OTHER STORIES

Edited by Barbara Ireson

What if you don't want to fight? What if you've stolen another boy's balaclava and want to give it back but don't dare? And what do you do when your mother makes you take a bright blue bag to school when everyone else's is greeny-brown? Here is a collection of twelve stories about school by such well-known writers as Robin Klein, Margaret Joy, Sylvia Woods and many more.

THE BIG PINK

Ann Pilling

Straight from her friendly local comprehensive, Angela is plunged into the alien life of her aunt's boarding school for girls. Overweight and horribly self-conscious, she immediately attracts the disapproval of Auntie Pat and the suspicions of the girls in her dormitory. But she finds allies in the school's more colourful characters, and her secret talent wins her the admiration of Sebastian, the teenage grandson of the school's benefactor. But still nothing she does will please Auntie Pat!

MAGGIE AND ME

Ted Staunton

Maggie's always got some brilliant plan — and Cyril inevitably has to help her. Whether it's getting back at the school bully or swapping places for piano lessons, these best friends are forever having adventures. Poor Cyril! Life without Maggie would be an awful lot easier, but then it would be much more boring. What would he do if she ever moved away? Here are ten stories about the intrepid duo.